For Linus
V.C. and C.F.

First published in 2001 by David & Charles Children's Books
This paperback edition published in 2010 for
Bookstart
by
Gullane Children's Books
185 Fleet Street, London, EC4A 2HS
www.gullanebooks.com

2 4 6 8 10 9 7 5 3 1

Text © Vicki Churchill 2001
Illustrations © Charles Fuge 2001

The right of Vicki Churchill and Charles Fuge to be identified as the author and illustrator
of this work has been asserted by them in accordance with the Copyright, Designs, and Patents Act, 1988.

A CIP record for this title is available from the British Library.

ISBN: 978-1-86233-844-9

Printed and bound in China

Sometimes I Like to Curl up in a Ball

Written by **Vicki Churchill**

Illustrated by **Charles Fuge**

GULLANE
CHILDREN'S BOOKS

Sometimes I like
to curl up in a ball,
So no one can see me
because I'm so small.

Sometimes I like to jump high as I can,

To see how much
noise I can make
when I land.

Sometimes I like to scream ever so loud,

Not that I'm cross, I just like how it sounds.

Sometimes I like to just
walk round and round,

I pigeon step, pigeon step,
till I fall down.

Sometimes I like to stand still as a tree,

And watch everyone rush around about me.

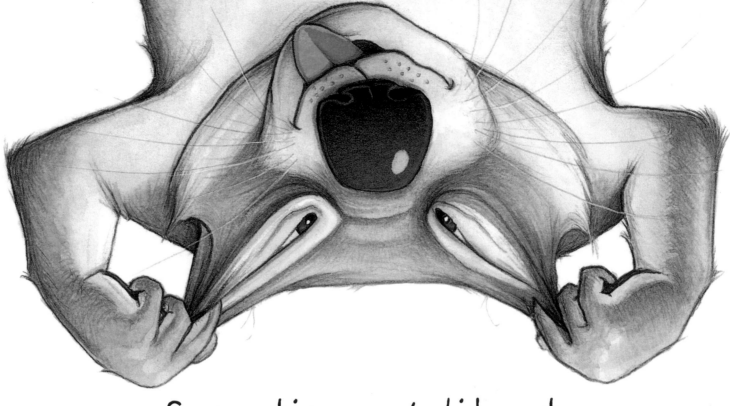

Sometimes I like to
poke out my tongue,

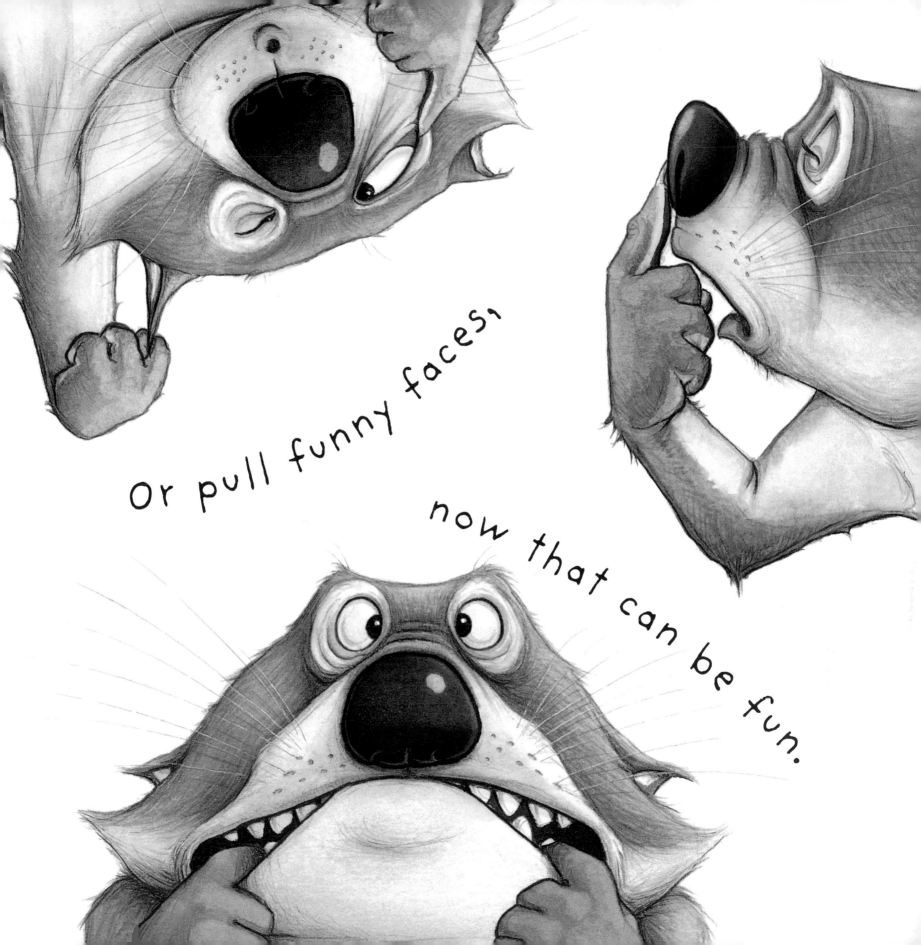

Or pull funny faces, now that can be fun.

Sometimes I like to get
in a real mess,

With mud on my feet and
my hands and my chest.

Sometimes I like to run
ever so fast,

I sometimes come first,
but I sometimes come last.

But when the day ends
and the sun starts to fall,
Then I do what I do best of all.
I find somewhere soft,
somewhere cosy and small...

...And that's where I like to curl up in a ball.